DREAM WARRIOR

AN ASHWOOD CHRONICLES STORY

R.L. SMITH

Dream Warrior
1st Edition
Copyright ©2023 R.L. Smith

Cover art & design by R.L. Smith
Book design & layout by R.L. Smith

Edited by Brittany M Smith & Megan Wass

ISBN: 979-8-9885357-0-6

I want to dedicate this book to my wife, Brittany Smith. Your support and strength have been amazing.

I love you more than you know, and you mean far more to me than I will ever be able to express!

Oppressive mist swirled all around her, making it impossible to see more than a couple of feet ahead. She could feel the warmth of a bright light shining on her back, a stark contrast to the cold void of darkness drawing her forward.

The compulsion to walk into the darkness was strong, yet she stayed where she was to keep the cold at bay. The warmth was nice, so why not soak it up before venturing forward?

One step forward was as far as she travelled before a soft, almost inaudible voice called to her. It sounded as if it was coming from the source of the light, and the message was simple.

"Don't go that way. Turn toward me and follow my voice."

She paused and made a half-turn in the direction of the voice. The light was blinding in her peripheral vision, but its warmth felt so good. She raised her hand to shield her eyes and began to fully turn her body toward the light. That's when the other voice spoke to her, from the darkness. She froze.

"You're going to listen to that old fool? You really desire the darkness. It fascinates you, thrills you. Come to me and let me show you all that you desire."

This voice was louder, bold and smooth, yet there was a bite to the words. Alarm bells rang in her head, but the desire to follow the second voice was so strong that she was willing to brave the cold.

Slowly, the light faded as she took her first steps toward the darkness. Vestiges of the words *"don't go that way"* clung to her memory even as the cold washed over her, numbing her senses.

She stopped walking. The acrid taste of fear on her tongue grew so strong that she thought she would be sick. She spun around to make her way back to the light, and the warmth it promised, but was met with a twisted iron gate blocking her path.

She grabbed the cold, black metal and pulled herself closer. The once warm and bright light was now a pinprick in the distance. However, she thought she could still hear the soft voice calling to her...*"follow my voice*"…but it was so hard to hear, and she was so cold that it was becoming difficult to move at all.

"How can I follow your voice with the gate blocking my path?"

The words were difficult to get out. They were thick in her mouth and stuck to her tongue. She wasn't sure if she could even be heard, or if she had spoken at all.

Something was very wrong. The darkness behind her grew even darker as she felt a twisted, evil presence approaching her. She felt small in comparison to the immense shadow that was passing over her as this unseen stalker grew closer. The cold intensified.

Breathing became difficult as the air felt like it was freezing in her lungs. All she could do was reach through the gate and stretch her hand toward the light. Icy fingers wrapped around her other arm and she was jerked away from the gate with a violence she had never felt before.

Pain shot through her arm as her shoulder became dislocated from its socket. She didn't have the breath to cry out, so the pain was released in silent tears staining her face.

The grip on her arm grew impossibly tight, and the once bold and smooth voice began speaking to her again. This time was different, though. This time it made her skin crawl with fear, rather than thrill. It took on a tone of harshness and sounded like many voices speaking at once. The voice had become a terrifying chorus of horror.

"You fool! You could have turned away and never entered this abyss of damnation. The choice was yours alone. You chose me, and now...you're mine!"

She was being spun around to face the owner of the horrific voice. Out of sheer terror she forced her eyes shut. She was sure this was the end for her, and she didn't want to see it.

Kara's eyes opened, expecting to see an image of terror, but she was greeted with a view of her bedroom ceiling. It had been a dream. Actually, it had been the same dream she had been having for weeks now.

Each time felt as real as the first. She never realized she was dreaming until she woke up covered in sweat. It always left her feeling shaken for a few hours, and gradually faded as the day played out. This time felt different. It felt more ominous.

She made a mental note to talk to her counselor about this at her appointment today. She glanced at the clock on her nightstand and realized she didn't have a lot of time before that appointment.

"Well, let's get this day started with a hot shower and a quick breakfast." Kara looked at her loyal companion as though she expected an answer.

Blue just cocked his head to the side and proceeded to stretch at her bed side. He was a big pit bull with floppy ears and a whip for a tail.

She scratched his head as she filled his food bowl. He blinked big, blue eyes in gratitude and licked her hand before he chowed down on his breakfast.

———✦✦✦———

Kara wrapped a towel around her body as she stepped out of the shower. She had hoped the hot steam and water would have washed away the heaviness she felt, but when she wiped away the condensation from the mirror, the dark circles under her eyes told a different story.

Her eyes were bright blue with flecks of gold mixed in. When the light hit them exactly right, the gold appeared to glow a vibrant amber. She thought her eyes were her best feature, but lately they didn't seem as bright as they had been before the dreams started.

She pulled her thick, brown hair into a high ponytail, put some lip gloss on plump lips, and headed to the kitchen.

"No time to glam this morning, Kara. Time to get this day over and done with." She spoke the words just to fill the silence.

She was alone in the house, like most days. Her foster parents were nice, but they were never there. They both had corporate careers and poured almost all of their time into work.

They always made sure that she had what she needed, though, and she was grateful for that. When they weren't working, they were involved at their church. Kara could appreciate their dedication, but she had decided many years ago that religion wasn't her thing.

Religion was what had landed her in the foster system to begin with, and there was no way she was ever going to relive that. Her parents had been religious zealots. They were both physically and emotionally abusive. They would shove "God" and "faith" down her throat every time they spoke to her, all while beating her severely for *sins* she had apparently committed.

The final straw came when they nearly drowned her in her own bathtub, trying to get the demons out of her. In Kara's mind, they were the demons. They appeared to be holy to everyone else, but lived drunken, abusive lives privately.

She went to school the next day and told her counselor everything, and declared she would never go back to that house again.

That had been her eighth-grade year. She graduated high school two weeks ago and was turning 18 in a few days. That meant she was aging out of the foster system and would be on her own. Today was the last session with the counselor she had been seeing all through high school and hopefully the close on this chapter of her life. She was looking forward to a fresh start.

"Be good, Blue." Kara said as she headed out the door. "I'll be home soon."

With that, Kara got in her car and headed to her counseling session.

She turned up the music to drown out the doubts swirling in her mind as she turned her car onto the street.

Dr. Barclay, Kara's counselor, took notes as he asked questions. "Your dream sounds spiritual in nature. Have you attended a church service or anything recently?"

"No. Church was my parents' thing, and we know how that ended. My foster parents go to church occasionally, but it's not for me. I try to stay away from the religious stuff." Kara shifted her position in the chair.

She was certain the counselor was interpreting her constant fidgeting as nerves, or some other psychological ailment, but the reality was the chair just wasn't comfortable.

In fact, the whole office gave an uncomfortable vibe. It was decorated in a contemporary style with a lot of black and white. Abstract art adorned the walls, and the air had an almost too clean smell to it, most likely the result of the air purifier humming in the background.

"So, you had no control in this dream?" Dr. Barclay leaned forward.

"No." Kara gave a small shake of her head in conjunction with her answer.

The fact that Kara had been able to realize she was dreaming and exercise some amount of control in her dreams had come up in multiple sessions. This was something she had been able to do even as a child.

Dr. Barclay had told her it was a form of lucid dreaming, and that some people were able to do that, or at least dream that they were doing it. The jury was still out if this phenomenon was a real occurrence or just an extension of the subconscious.

"It seems that your lack of control in the dream may be the result of feeling like your life is out of control. You do have a lot happening at once. No one could blame you if you felt like you had no control."

The counselor put down the notepad and looked directly at Kara. The next words out of his mouth were not what she had expected to hear. However, they struck a chord of truth deep within her.

"Kara, I feel like you're only coming to these sessions out of a sense of routine at this point. I think you know what needs to be done in order to move forward. The question is, are you ready to do that?"

Kara blinked back the tears that were threatening to spill. "I'm not sure what you mean," she lied.

"I think you do. You don't have anyone to tell you what to do going forward, and that scares you." He took a pause before continuing, measuring Kara's response.

"You will be responsible for the direction your life takes now, and that is new and frightening. Your fears have manifested themselves in a creative way, but the good news is that there aren't actual monsters waiting to get you, just new experiences." He smiled. "Look at it as the fresh start you've been looking forward to."

Kara let a tear escape and roll down her cheek. She lowered her head and asked the question that had plagued her most of her life.

"What if I live my life never measuring up? I mean, my parents obviously didn't love me. My foster parents are nice enough, but they aren't really involved. I just feel...*alone.*"

Dr. Barclay let the silence stretch for a moment before answering. He weighed his words carefully, not wanting to bring any more pain into Kara's life.

"Kara, being alone isn't always a bad thing. I know it feels like it, but it isn't. It can allow us to focus on ourselves and heal from past hurts. We all need that from time to time." He reached across the desk and gave her hand a gentle squeeze. "Besides, it's often when we feel hopeless and alone that we begin to realize that there is hope, and that we aren't really as alone as we feel."

Kara knew he was right. She could feel the truth of what he was saying. It didn't make it easy, but it gave her the resolve to turn her life into something that would make a difference. She wouldn't allow the abuse of her parents to hold her back any longer.

"Thanks for being here for me over these four years of my life. You're right. It's time to face the big, scary world and the fact that I'm officially on my own."

With that Kara walked out of the office and into the world with a slightly different outlook on her situation. She smiled as she got in her car and left for home.

If only she'd known just how scary the world truly is, she might have talked with the doctor a little longer. She was going to find out, and it was going to change her forever.

Kara stretched out on the sofa with Blue curled up at her feet. She was finishing Narnia for the 11th time. It was one of her favorites, but her eyes were getting heavy, and she drifted off to sleep without realizing it.

She was in her dream again. The mist was swirling around her. Warm light was to her back, and the cold darkness was once again in front of her. She knew she should turn towards the light. She knew what awaited her in the dark, but she couldn't will her body to turn. She still couldn't control this dream.

She felt as if she was being pulled along the path deeper into the darkness. She wanted to turn and go toward the light, but she wasn't strong enough to fight the force that held her captive. The sudden feeling of total helplessness was overwhelming. Tears began to roll down her face as she remembered what waited for her in the dark.

She was finally able to turn toward the light, but the twisted black gate blocked her path just as it had the last time. The icy metal bit into her palms as she grabbed the bars and tried to pry them open enough to squeeze through. She was just too weak. The cold darkness had drained her of any strength she may have once had.

She could feel the terrible presence approaching her from behind. She could hear the words echoing in her mind.

"*You chose me! Now, you're mine!*"

Kara managed to speak this time. She wasn't sure if she was gaining a small amount of control or if this was just part of the dream.

"No! I don't choose you. I didn't want to take this path! I was pulled here against my will.*"*

The grip on her shoulder loosened. The chorus of voices spoke to her.

"*Have it your way you pathetic meat puppet.*" Each word, dripping with hatred, was spat at her. "*You're only fooling yourself, though. You'll see!*" The voice trailed off and, with it, the overwhelming fear abated.

The iron gate groaned as the door swung open. Kara stepped through the opening quickly, fearful it may slam shut at any moment. One thing was certain, she was in control of her dream again. She began the journey toward the pin prick of light that had once been so warm and bright.

No more than three steps into her journey, she stopped abruptly. The fog began to swirl. Figures began to slowly form and appear all around her. They were so black, it was almost as if they were voids in the landscape, except for the fact that they were moving toward her, and quickly!

There were four large humanoid shapes closing in on her position. However, these weren't normal human shapes. They were at least eight feet tall, maybe taller. Well-muscled bodies did nothing to slow them down and did everything to make them appear more intimidating.

"It's okay. This is fine. This is my dream and I'm in control here." She spoke aloud in an attempt to calm her nerves. It didn't help.

She could feel the ground tremble beneath her feet as the colossal figures got closer. They were just shadows with no facial features. Shadows didn't make the ground shake, though. Shadows couldn't hurt you, and something was telling Kara that whatever these were *could.*

Kara closed her eyes and willed the familiar transformation to happen. When she opened her eyes again, she looked down to see that she was wearing her dream armor, as she liked to call it.

The armor was ebony platemail. Intricate designs were etched into the breast plate, shoulder pauldrons, gauntlets, and boots. Black leather pants were hidden underneath the armor plates covering her legs.

Each shoulder pauldron was fastened to the chest plate with an ornate amethyst crystal that had been cut into a perfect circle. The long sword strapped to her back also had an amethyst crystal adorning the hilt. Kara wrapped her hand around the hilt of that sword and drew it from the sheath. She was ready for battle.

"Trust me, Kara... Call on me for help. You're not strong enough on your own for this battle."

It was the voice from the light. She could almost *feel* the words, rather than hear them. She paused for only a moment before deciding that she could handle these shadow people on her own. After all, it was *her* dream, and she was in control at last. She was going to enjoy this.

She reached the first of the shadow people and gave a baseball style swing with the sword. The shadow person was cleaved in half at the waist and dissipated into a black vapor before either half hit the ground.

The second shadow was quickly approaching on her left. Kara threw herself into a spin and lopped off its head. Again, it turned into black vapor before hitting the ground. Kara didn't have time to catch her breath before the third shadow was upon her. She had just enough time to roll under the shadow's grasping arms. However, that roll put her directly in front of the fourth entity.

This foe seemed taller than the rest. It appeared to be almost ten feet tall. The height wasn't the only difference. An otherworldly face was visible on this one. Cruel, seething hatred twisted its features in a way that brought dread into Kara. She wasn't fast enough to dodge this attack.

"Call out to me. Trust me." The voice from the light called out just as Kara was struck hard by the shadow creature.

She had managed to roll her body slightly before impact. The giant shadow's fist caught her squarely in the shoulder, shattering her armor and sending her flying into the air. Her shoulder was crushed, and her arm was broken.

She landed hard on the ground several feet away. The impact drove the wind from her lungs, leaving her dazed and confused. She was able to lift her head just in time to see a massive, black foot crashing down on her head. Kara let out a smothered scream, and then her world faded to black.

Kara opened her eyes to see Blue standing over her with his head tilted to the side. She realized that she had fallen off the sofa. The throbbing pain in her head was likely the result of hitting it during the fall. It had all been a dream. However, this dream had left its mark in more ways than one.

"It's okay, boy. I'm fine." She scratched behind Blue's ears and was rewarded with a lick up her cheek.

The pain in her head was already starting to go away, but her right shoulder was a different story. It felt as if she had been hit by a truck. In the dream she had been hit by a giant shadow-*thing*, but this was the real world with no giant shadows in sight.

She put her hand against her shoulder and winced at the pain. Just touching it hurt. She pulled her shirt down over her shoulder to get a look and was shocked to see a nasty bruise spread across the area.

The bruise had formed much too soon to be from the fall off the sofa, not to mention she hadn't fallen far enough to leave a mark like that. The sofa was only about two feet off of the floor.

There were similar occurrences that had happened a few times throughout Kara's life. She had awakened from a dream, sporting injuries she received while dreaming, on more than one occasion. A bruise here. A scratch or cut there. However, it had been years since she had experienced anything like this. She was unable to rationalize why it had started happening again.

When she was younger it was easier to believe that her ability to control her dreams was supernatural in nature. It was easier for her to accept that the things that happened to her in her dreams could also affect her when she was awake. It all seemed exciting, like one of the many fantasy stories she liked to read. It was an escape from the horror of her real life.

Then, she turned 12 and stopped believing in the supernatural. She was growing up and things had continued down a bad road with her home life. As a result, she wasn't able to control her dreams as frequently, and she never had any lingering effects from them. She just lived a regular life, albeit a life that was beginning to be dominated by mental and physical abuse.

Now she was starting to wonder if perhaps it had been real all along. She was almost 18, and it was starting to happen again. Kara thought she had a fairly good idea who the voices in her dream belonged to, and she wasn't sure if she liked the implications.

She always believed it was easier for her to ignore religion because of what she went through as a child. She had been told, multiple times, the fact that her parents had been terrible representatives of Christianity didn't mean there wasn't truth in the teachings of it.

If the voices were who she thought they were, then this line of thought certainly warranted deeper consideration. Maybe people were right. Maybe her parents were the ones that forced her upon the dark path that she dreamed about so frequently. Maybe that *was* Satan talking to her from the darkness, and if so, that meant it was *God* calling to her from the light.

Just thinking the thoughts brought on a headache. She had spent so many years putting all the religious nonsense out of her life. Now, it seemed like she was being forced to deal with it, whether she wanted to or not. Sure, she could continue to ignore it and go on with her life. However, if what she was experiencing in her dreams was real, how dangerous would it be to continue living like God and Satan didn't exist?

One thing was certain. She wasn't going to figure it out in the next five minutes, so she decided to make a sandwich to quiet the growling of her stomach.

Kara was putting the top slice of bread on her sandwich when Blue let out a low rumbling growl. She was used to Blue being right beside her anytime she went into the kitchen. He was always hoping she would drop something, but he had never acted this way.

Blue was intently staring out the window of her back door with his teeth bared, ears pinned back, and tail straight up. The growl increased in volume until it erupted into a viscous bark. The barking didn't stop until Kara put her hand on his head.

"What is it, boy? What's out there?" Kara's voice did nothing to relax Blue's posture, but he was silent.

Kara walked to the window and peered through the pane of glass separating her from the outside world. Aside from the chill that ran down her spine, she didn't see anything out of the ordinary.

Her eyes scanned the back yard. Green grass, blue sky, and trees were all that met her vision. Her nose wrinkled at the faint scent of sulfur hanging in the air. Shrugging her shoulders, she turned from the window and went into the living room to eat her sandwich and watch some television.

"Come on, boy." Blue gave one more low bark and then turned and followed Kara.

Perhaps, if Kara had been dreaming, she would have seen the set of eyes that was watching her from the tree line. Perhaps, if she had been dreaming, she would have seen the large body made of dark shadow that those eyes belonged to. However, Kara was awake and didn't notice what her animal companion was able to see.

Night was coming. Tonight, she would meet her unseen watcher in another reality. Tonight, her dream would become a living nightmare.

DREAM WARRIOR

34

The room grew dark when Kara
clicked the TV off. At some point, and
she wasn't sure when, the sun had gone
down. Reaching over to turn on the
lamp, she saw that Blue was asleep,
curled just beneath her feet, with her

copy of Narnia halfway visible under his body.

She didn't want to wake him, so she allowed her eyes to slowly drift over to the Bible laying on the end table next to her. She reached out to take hold of it, and then stopped just short of actually touching it.

She had been physically struck by this book, or a version of it, many times. Her father would hit her across the face with his thick leather Bible as he screamed profanity-laced accusations towards her. But her father wasn't here now, and she was desperate to understand what was happening to her.

The leather was cool as she picked the Bible up from the end table. She flipped through the pages and came to a stop at the beginning of the book of Matthew. She began reading and allowed herself to be completely open-minded.

She read about the birth of the Messiah. She read about the life of the

Messiah, and all of the extraordinary miracles he had performed. She read through his words and sermons and, for the first time, heard the love that was behind his words. Even the tough messages were given out of love.

Then she read about his death. It was a horrible, brutal, violent death that she couldn't fathom. What struck her was the fact that he had suffered that death willingly. For her.

Finally, she read about his resurrection, ascension, and his promise to return. She had read through the entire book of Matthew before she'd realized it. She glanced down at Blue, asleep at her feet again, then a quick glance at the clock revealed it was almost two in the morning.

"Come on, Blue. It's way past bedtime."

Kara opened the back door to allow Blue to do his business one more time before bed. She wrapped her arms around her to ward off the chill in the air. She was looking up at the sky, pondering all she had just read. She allowed her mind to replay some of the passages.

Her train of thought stopped on the story of the man in the tombs, and the legion of demons that possessed him. Kara shivered and pulled her arms a little tighter at the thought of that. She wondered if the shadows in her dreams were demons as well, assuming everything she had read was true.

Suddenly the dark seemed a little darker, and a feeling of dread slammed into her stomach like a truck. She couldn't get back inside fast enough.

"Come, Blue." She turned and didn't look back, shutting the door behind her once Blue was inside.

With all the doors and windows locked, Kara finally allowed herself to go to bed. She pulled the covers just a little closer tonight, unable to shake the chill in her bones. The cold she felt reminded her of the cold darkness in her dreams.

"God, if you're up there, please help me. I feel like I'm losing my mind. I know I haven't talked to you in a long time, and I'm not sure you can actually hear me, but I need you. If you're real."

Kara's eyes closed, after the first prayer she had prayed in many years, and almost immediately she was back in her dream. Light was shining bright behind her, and the cold darkness was once again in front of her. She already knew she didn't want to walk the dark path, yet she felt herself being pulled forward.

Kara grit her teeth under the pressure of digging her heels into the ground in an attempt to stop her forward momentum. She was at the point of giving up the struggle, and allowing herself to be pulled into the dark, when the voice from the light spoke directly to her.

"Kara, turn toward me and follow my voice."

"How exactly do I do that when I can't break free from *whatever* is pulling me away?!"

"All you have to do is ask me."

Kara gave up her struggle and dropped to her knees. The forward momentum tore her jeans and scraped her knees. Clenching her teeth to fight the pain, Kara cried out as loud as she could.

"Help me! Please help me!"

Immediately, she came to a stop. She could see the twisted black gate ahead of her. It was nice to be on this side of it for a change. However, that didn't take long to change.

The low rumble of the gate opening filled Kara with dread. An exceptionally large shadow was approaching her at an alarming speed. This one was different, bigger if that was possible. She knew instinctively that the terrible voice from the darkness belonged to this fiend closing in on her.

Kara willed her armor into place, but nothing happened. As the shadow grew closer, she tried and tried, to no avail, to get the armor to appear. When the features of the twisted face came into view, she shut her eyes out of sheer reflex.

"You're not going to be able to fight this battle, Kara. Just trust me. Open your eyes and relax. It's time to face your enemy."

The soft voice from the light brought waves of peace that washed over Kara's being. Fear subsided as warmth flooded her. She opened her eyes in obedience to the voice. A small crack formed in that shield of peace once she locked eyes with the demon before her, but the shield held.

The hulking form that stood before her had to be at least 12 feet tall. It resembled a man, but the yellow eyes with slits for pupils, scales covering two thirds of its body, and the three pairs of translucent wings sprouting out of its back, indicated that it was something more than a man.

The thing before her seemed to pulsate with an unearthly glow that changed in hue with each pulse. He leaned down to be at eye level with Kara and the pulse took on a harsh red glow. Kara's nose wrinkled at the strong sulfurous odor assaulting her nostrils.

"That is close enough, Azazel!"

The once-soft voice from the light sounded as if it were roaring thunder. The ground shook under the command of the voice, and Kara found herself face down, not out of fear, but out of respect.

The strange-looking snake-man thing, Azazel, stopped dead in his tracks. He strained against an unseen force, as if trying to progress, but could not move.

"Arise, Kara." The voice was soft, loving, and peaceful.

Kara stood up on trembling legs and glanced at Azazel. She shifted her eyes back to her feet as she managed to mutter a question, unable to look into his serpentine eyes.

"Who... *what* are you?"

"*I am many things. I have many names. You humans have called me Lucifer, as well as Samael, Mastema, Gadreel, Zeus, The Devil, and Satan, among others. Are you catching on yet?*"

Kara didn't move. She didn't breathe, and she didn't dare look up.

"*Look at me you pathetic mortal!*" Harsh red light flashed like lightning as the chorus of voices spoke.

Kara glanced up in time to see the being in front of her begin to shift. It changed, in an almost mesmerizing way, from the terrifying visage of a six-winged snake-man into the most handsome man that Kara had ever seen. She couldn't help but blush at the immediate attraction she felt.

"*Is this better for your weak mind?*" The voice was smooth and human.

Kara looked into the warm chestnut eyes that were now locked onto her in an alarmingly hypnotic fashion. Strands of his dark hair blew in a breeze that could not be felt. Azazel still pulsated with light, only it was a warm amber color, like the light of the sun. She could almost make out something that looked like scales as the light shifted across his body.

"Is this really the Devil?" Kara asked the voice from the light while trying to avert her gaze from the beautiful being in front of her.

"*Yes.*" It was the only word the soft voice spoke.

"Then that means you're..." Kara didn't finish her sentence.

"*Yes, Kara. I am Yahweh Elohim, the true living God that you read about earlier tonight. I am the same God that you prayed to for help, and I heard every word."*

Kara had turned her back on Azazel now and was facing the light with tears streaming down her face. Azazel strained against the force holding him in place, wishing he could snatch her away from Yahweh's presence and end her existence. He would have to wait for a more opportune time.

"*Don't turn your back on me!*" The voice wasn't human any longer, and Kara suspected that Azazel wasn't either.

"I'm so sorry for not believing for so long!" Kara spoke directly to the light now, unable to see anything beyond the blinding brilliance.

"I'm sorry." Kara fell to her knees, weeping unashamedly.

"*Shut your mouth, girl! I'll destroy you!*" The sound was of a million voices screaming in agony, and Kara couldn't help but to jump at the sudden outburst.

"*That is enough, Azazel! Be silent!*"

Azazel found himself unable to speak. The pulsating light around his body grew in intensity until Kara could see the vibrant red in the corners of her vision.

"Please God, don't let him hurt me."

"The Messiah you read about earlier is my son. Yeshua, or Jesus as you read, is your pathway to me. You must decide if you believe in him and want to follow his ways. Only then will you fully understand all that is happening to you."

Yahweh released the spiritual muzzle from the mouth of Azazel to allow him to tempt Kara. She must choose, of her own will, to reject Satan and follow the path she was destined for.

"Oh, here we go again. Follow me, Kara. Don't follow the big scary guy." Azazel rolled his eyes. *"He'll lead you to the bad place."* Satan continued his mocking.

Kara turned to face the terrible visage of Azazel. He looked larger and more terrifying than before.

How is that even possible?

He emitted a pulse of red so harsh that Kara could only make out the fierce eyes that were locked onto her.

"*Kara, don't listen to the old man. He will stifle you with rules and regulations.*" He began to change his appearance into that of Kara's biological father. "*Remember, this guy was a Christian. How did that work out for you?*"

Kara closed her eyes tight to block out the image in front of her. The memories came crashing down, threatening to bury her.

The beatings that drove her to hate religion, and eventually, God. The constant emotional abuse that caused her to seek escape through pills. She remembered all the times that she lashed out in hatred to those who tried to show her love. Her distrust of people's motives. The sudden rush of all those memories and emotions was suffocating, almost unbearable.

She had thought it was all due to the man who now stood before her. However, now she wasn't sure. She felt her own part of the blame so acutely in the presence of Yahweh. It was her choice all along how she'd dealt with what she was going through.

She could have asked God for help, but she chose to hate him and shut him out. She wasn't going to make that same mistake again. She would choose differently this time.

"Yeah, I'm not so sure he was a Christian. I think he hid behind religion to justify his actions. I think he probably followed you." Kara lifted her chin and looked directly at Azazel. "I'm not going to be manipulated and controlled by you!"

"*I will destroy you. I will take away everything you have. You will die by my hand, Kara! Remember this moment!*" Azazel roared in his multi-chorus voice.

Kara turned her back on him, confident that Yahweh would protect her.

"I choose your son, Jesus. I want to live my life for you. I want to live my life differently than I have up to this point. If you'll have me, I'll serve you."

"I will have you. I have big plans for you, Kara. I will make it all clear to you in time, but for now, just trust me."

Azazel was furious. His roaring and cursing was constant throughout the entire exchange between Yahweh and Kara.

Sulfurous fumes were pluming from his nostrils. Violent red flashed all about his body and his six wings, no longer translucent, unfurled into a massive wingspan of black feathers.

A hand reached out of the light and touched Kara on her forehead. She was immediately dressed in her dream armor with her sword in her hand. However, it was different.

White light radiated from the armor and her sword's blade was aflame. She almost dropped it out of shock but managed to keep her grip on it as she turned back around to face Azazel.

"I may not be able to harm you here, but a time is coming when this world and your waking world will begin to merge, and then I will destroy you as I have promised." Azazel lifted off the ground with one swoop of his wings. *"Remember my words, Kara. I will taste your blood when that day comes, and you will fall by my hand."*

In a blinding flash of red, Azazel was gone, leaving only a streak of red in the sky as he went back into the darkness beyond the black gate.

"What did he mean about this world and the waking world merging?"

"This world, this dream, isn't what you think it is. Your dreams, some of them, are your gateway into the spiritual realm. This is a real place and

you have been given a great spiritual gift that enables you to engage in spiritual warfare on a whole new level."

The landscape around Kara began to shift. What once appeared to be a void, other than Yahweh's light, began to form a landscape. Myriads of paths were visible, some blocked by gates, and others with unrestricted access. Hills in the distance were obscured by fog. She could make out crops of trees, and high above them there appeared to be floating islands with landscapes of their own.

Kara had never seen anything so beautiful and terrifying at the same time. It felt as if reality was being shattered with every new sight that she took in. She was snapped out of her reverie by the unmistakable voice of Yahweh Elohim.

"There is coming a day that Azazel will have free reign in the physical world. In fact, the merger, as he put it, isn't far away. What once was

bound to this realm will be granted access to the physical world in ways not previously permitted."

"Why is he allowed to do this?"

"*It is part of my plan, just as you are part of my plan.*"

BANG...BANG...BANG

Yahweh's voice began to sound distant. She could feel herself trying to wake up. She fought against it. She needed to stay just a little longer. She still needed answers.

"*I will reveal what needs to be revealed to you as you need it. You will have to trust me with the rest.*"

BANG...BANG...BANG

"I do."

"*Then, it's time for you to wake up. You have a guest at your door.*"

Kara's eyes fluttered open, and she sat up in bed. Blue was standing at her bedroom door with his fur bristled and ears pinned back. The knocking at her front door had him agitated.

BANG...BANG...BANG

"I'm coming!" Kara scratched Blue behind the ears on her way out of the bedroom. "Come on, boy. Let's see who it is."

Peeking through the side window, Kara saw a man standing at her front door. His slacks and button-down matched his neatly combed hair. He held a flyer.

"Can I help you?" Kara asked through a small gap in the door.

"Good morning. I hope I didn't wake you. My name is Tommy, and I'm with Grace Community Church. I am just out inviting people to join us in service this Sunday." He smiled warmly and paused for Kara to speak.

"Oh, okay." Kara opened the door to a more social distance and returned his smile. "Thank you. I would love to visit."

"That's great news. Yeah, I normally skip over this and a few other houses on this street because I know they belong to another church, but something told me I should stop here today."

"I'm glad you did. Thank you." Kara started to close the door, but Tommy started to speak again.

"By the way, the church is always open during business hours. Our associate pastor is usually in the office as well, if you wanted to come by and check things out before Sunday."

"I'll keep that in mind. Thank you."

"Enjoy the rest of your day. See you Sunday." Tommy turned to leave.

"Have a good day." Kara closed the door and stood there a few moments processing her thoughts.

Okay, God. I get the message. I'm going to check this church out.

She paused her thoughts, expecting to hear the warm voice from her dream. She was met with silence and felt a prick of disappointment. She hadn't been able to get that voice out of her mind and had come to find comfort in it.

Last night was definitely more than a dream. I'm going to trust you, like you said, but I need some direction. This is scary stuff.

When she didn't get a response, she went into her room to get her day started. She caught a glimpse of the Bible on her nightstand on her way to the shower. Before she realized it, she was curled up in bed and had started reading.

She started at the front this time with Genesis. With plans to read one chapter and then get ready and go about her day, she began to read. When she stopped, she had read six chapters and had a headache. She had more questions than answers at this point and decided that she would go check out that church. Maybe the pastor could provide some answers.

Kara stood on the doorstep of Grace Community Church. She dried her sweaty palms on her jeans and opened the door. The entry appeared to be empty. Kara was turning to leave when a voice startled her.

"Hi."

Kara turned to see a man who looked to be in his mid-fifties standing in the doorway that led to the sanctuary. He smiled at her with a smile that reached his bright blue eyes as well.

"I'm afraid the secretary is away for a moment. Did you need an appointment?"

"Actually, I just came by to check out the church. Someone came by my house this morning and invited me. He said the associate pastor is always here." Kara returned his smile to be polite.

"Ah, yes. Well, that's me. I am the associate pastor. The name's Joshua. You can call me Josh if you prefer. You have some questions for me, then?" He gave Kara a knowing look with his piercing blue eyes.

"Um, well yes, actually I do. How did you know?"

"I knew you were coming. I saw you in a dream."

"I'm sorry. You saw me in a…"

"I know, it sounds strange. Please, let me explain." He motioned to the back pew of the sanctuary.

"Honestly, when it comes to dreams, nothing really surprises me anymore. This should be interesting." Kara followed the pastor into the sanctuary and took a seat across from him.

Somewhere at the end of a dark alley, several young lives hung in the balance. Behind the door to an old, abandoned warehouse were several rusty, human-sized cages. Those cages were not empty. Many of the girls had ceased to cry for help, but the occasional cry or whimper would escape their dry throats.

They were barely dressed, barely fed, and had almost lost hope. One girl, however, continued to pray for rescue. Those prayers amused the many unseen occupants of the warehouse.

Invisible to the humans in the cages, yellow eyes watched them from each corner of the room. Those eyes belonged to large, eight-to-ten-feet tall bodies made up of dense shadow. They watched with incredible hatred for the humans in the cages, and took intense pleasure in their suffering. They served as guards, ever watchful, and always present.

A shift in the atmosphere was beginning to transpire, a merger of two worlds. Soon, they would no longer remain unseen. They would be able to take the forms of times past, forms of those from darker times. For now, they would keep watch and alert their chief if the girl showed up.

She was a fledgling warrior, still learning the ropes, but she did pose a threat. They would take that threat seriously. They had no desire to go to the abyss before the appointed time.

Pastor Joshua and Kara had been talking for over an hour. Kara's mind was reeling from the information she had learned in such a short time.

She had told him about her dreams, and that she had always been able to exhibit some amount of control in them. She told him about her recent encounters with shadow beings in the dreams, and he confirmed that they were demons, just as she had suspected.

Joshua explained that demons were the spirits of the Nephilim she had read about in Genesis. He described the days of Noah in a way that she had never dreamed possible. He told her about the Nephilim, and the terrible things they brought upon humanity. The violence they had wrought was beyond her comprehension.

She learned that through the meddling of fallen angels and the Nephilim, many hybrid creatures had been introduced to humanity.

"Myths and legends that we grow up hearing about are based in reality. Most of what is taught as mythology, especially what gets labeled as Greek mythology, is actually ancient history.

Many legends, such as vampires, werewolves, and a whole host of creatures of the dark, have origins based in reality."

Kara ran her fingers through her hair and stared blankly at him after that last statement, feeling like she was in an episode of X-Files. She had believed these creatures were just fantasy, yet she knew that he was being truthful.

"I know it's a lot to take in." He gave her an apologetic look.

"That's an understatement." Kara ran her hand through her dark hair. "I'm beginning to get a headache. This is just so much to wrap my head around."

"Kara, it is especially important that you remain aware during this time. Now that you have been exposed to these spiritual forces, you are on their radar." He took on a more serious tone. "It sounds as though you have only interacted with them in the spirit realm through dreams. However, I believe that a time is coming when the spirit realm will merge with our physical realm."

Kara cut him short.

"That's exactly what Yahweh told me in the last dream I had. What does it mean?"

"Well, Scripture tells us that the last days will be like the days of Noah. I feel like we are quickly approaching the last days. If we aren't already in the very early stages, that time will be upon us very soon."

Joshua took a moment to compose his next words carefully. He didn't want to put all of this on Kara so quickly, but felt as though he had no choice. If he was right, and he thought he was, things were about to get bad for her very quickly.

"Listen, let's call it a day. I've hit you with a lot. This is a heavy subject, and you no doubt need time to process." Joshua stood and gestured for Kara to follow him. "I have something for you. I think it will help you with breaking down the information I've given you today."

They made their way out of the sanctuary and the Pastor led her to his office. The church was beautiful. Inspirational art hung on the walls of the hallway they walked down to reach his office. He opened the door at the end of the hallway and ushered Kara inside.

"Well, hi there." The voice belonged to a smiling middle-aged woman. The picture on the desk told Kara that this must be Joshua's wife.

"Hey." Kara returned the warm smile.

"I'm Martha. Joshua told me he was expecting a visitor today."

"My name is Kara. Yeah, I thought I would come by and see the church. I had some questions."

"Let me guess, the answers were more than you were expecting?"

"You could say that, yes."

"My Joshua has a tendency to answer questions in unexpected ways. Sometimes the truth is stranger than fiction." Martha gave a knowing look and patted Kara on the shoulder as she passed her. "I'll leave you to finish your conversation. It was nice to meet you."

"Nice to meet you."

Joshua unlocked a small closet behind his desk. He felt around on the top shelf until he found what he was looking for.

"Ah! Here we go."

Joshua held out a brown leather satchel for Kara to take.

"These should help you decipher the things we have discussed and give you a little more insight into what the days of Noah were like."

Kara took the satchel from him and glanced inside. She saw three leatherbound books, and could make out the name "Enoch" etched into the spine of one of them.

"I warn you, this stuff isn't for the faint of heart." Joshua smiled. "The Book of Enoch paints a pretty scary picture of the days of Noah."

"The Book of Enoch?"

"Yes. It used to be included in the original canon of Scripture. In fact, it still *is* included in many different Bibles. Various councils took it upon themselves to have it removed from the official canon sometime around the fifth Century AD. After you read it, and as you learn more, I think you will understand why certain groups didn't want everyone to have the knowledge it provides."

"Thank you." Kara slung the satchel over her shoulder. "I have a lot of homework to do, I think."

"You'll also find a copy of Jasher and Jubilees in there. All three books will help you get a more detailed view of the events that transpired in the book of Genesis, and what we may see some of in the days to come."

"Okay. I will get these back to you as soon as I'm done with them."

"No. Keep them. I have a feeling that you'll get more use out of those than I will at this point in my life. Besides, I have other copies, just none that appear to be as old as those."

"If you're sure?"

"I am." He smiled that warm fatherly smile and his blue eyes twinkled.

"Thank you, Joshua. I will take care of them." Kara returned his smile and turned to leave.

"If you have any questions, you know where to find me, Kara. However, I feel that we have very different paths for the near future. I will do what I can to share truth with those who will listen. You, though, I suspect will have a more *active* role to play."

The way he emphasized the word "active" caused Kara's stomach to sink. Mostly because she knew he was right. She wasn't sure if she would ever see

Joshua again after today, but she knew that he was put in her path for a reason.

He had revealed so much to her in such a short time. It was certainly not a coincidence that she came by the church today. Now, as she walked out of his office and down the hall, she could feel the weight of the information weighing heavily on her.

She knew she had a steep learning curve to overcome and that things were about to get very interesting in her life. Yet, she still felt a peace deep within her. She hadn't felt peace like this before.

Kara looked up at the sky on the way to her car. The sun was being swallowed by dark storm clouds. She couldn't help but feel that it was symbolic of what her world was about to become. Dark.

"Yahweh, I hope you can hear me. I'm going to need your help."

A low rumble of thunder was her only reply. She got in her car and headed back to her house. Her foster parents wouldn't be back for another week. She planned to make good use of the empty house, though. She had a lot of studying to do.

Kara couldn't see her invisible passenger, but his yellow eyes burned with hatred. He glanced at the satchel in the passenger side floor and vanished in a flash of harsh red light. He needed to report this latest development to his superior. The warrior was being equipped with the deadly weapon of knowledge.

That evening, Kara went through the motions of eating dinner, feeding Blue, taking a shower, and getting ready for bed. She couldn't get through the day fast enough. She said a prayer asking for help and guidance and then pulled the first volume from the satchel that Joshua had given her earlier that day.

She spent the next few hours reading through the leather-bound copy of Enoch. She read about giants so big that they began to consume everything, even each other. Under any other circumstances she would believe these things to be fairytales. However, deep inside, she knew better.

As Kara turned the last page of the book, she glanced at the clock. What had felt like only an hour or so had, in reality, been almost four hours. It was after two in the morning and Kara needed to get some rest. Blue slept in his usual spot at her feet. He stirred as she spoke a familiar phrase aloud.

"C'mon boy, let's go potty!"

Blue's ears perked up, and he headed toward the back door. Kara opened the door and stepped outside with her loyal companion. The air felt crisp against her skin, and she took a moment to enjoy the steady breeze. She could smell the rain it was bringing in, and started thinking about what she would wear to combat the wet weather tomorrow.

Her mind was quickly drawn away from thoughts about her wardrobe when the familiar prickling fear that she had experienced the other night washed over her. She could feel someone, or some*thing* watching her, pressing in on her chest and stealing the air from her lungs.

"Probably an animal, Kara. Don't get yourself too worked up."

No sooner than she finished the thought, the dark silhouette of a man caught her eye. He was standing in the tree line of the woods behind her house. He was partially skewed by the trees, but Kara could tell he was unnaturally tall. His limbs appeared to be too long for his body, and she thought she recognized the shape.

"Oh no!" Her heart banged against her ribcage like it was trying to escape. *"It looks like the shadow people from my dreams."*

As the realization hit her, Blue let out a low warning growl and had his attention fixed on the spot in the woods that Kara had been staring at. Blue began to bark, and the figure slipped behind a tree and out of Kara's vision.

"Come, boy." Kara patted her leg.

Once Blue was at her side, she examined the wood line a few more minutes. Seeing no movement, she led Blue back into the house and locked the door behind them.

"You saw it too, huh boy?"

She was met with a quizzical turn of his head that left his ears flopping. She scratched behind those ears and nearly fell over at the sudden sound of her phone ringing.

"Get it together, Kara. It's just your phone, you big scaredy cat."

She grabbed her phone from the kitchen counter and hit the green circle to answer the call.

"Hello?"

"Hello. Is this Kara?"

"Yes. Who is this?"

"Are you the foster child of Mr. and Mrs. Franks?"

"I am. Who is this?"

"This is Officer Nelson with the NYPD. I regret to inform you that your foster parents were involved in an accident. They didn't survive, ma'am. I'm sorry."

Kara slid down against the counter into a sitting position as she experienced what felt like the end of her world. Kara's foster parents were dead. She listened for what felt like hours as the person on the other end of the line explained to her what had happened.

"What? How?" Hot tears stung her eyes, but Kara tried to hold it together as the officer gave her the details.

"It appears they were on their way to the airport when they were struck head on by a drunk driver. They didn't suffer. We believe their death was instantaneous."

Kara felt the weight of his words in the pit of her stomach. She couldn't believe this was happening. Was it just a dream? A nightmare, perhaps? She couldn't form the thoughts necessary to come to terms with what she was hearing. A distant voice broke through her state of mind and called her back to the moment at hand.

"Ma'am? Are you still there?"

It wasn't a dream.

Kara blinked away tears and tried to compose herself before answering.

"Yes, I'm here. What should I do?"

"Someone from our local coroner's office will contact you to make arrangements to have their bodies sent back home. Do you know which funeral home in your area they wanted to use?

"Yes."

"I would contact them as soon as they open. Perhaps your foster parents had plans filed with them for an event such as this. They will be able to guide you through the process." The officer cleared his throat. "Again, I'm so sorry for your loss."

Kara hung up the phone and broke down into unrestrained sobbing. Blue curled up beside her, sensing her emotional state. She wrapped her arms around him and cried until she had nothing else left.

Kara waited for what felt like an eternity for the funeral home to open. After hanging up with them, Kara walked to her room. Her world was already being turned upside down, and now she was truly alone, the people she had loved, taken from her by a drunk driver.

She felt numb inside. She didn't know what to do, so she fell into bed and cried herself to sleep. She did not dream of Yahweh. She did not dream of Azazel.

Instead, she dreamed of car accidents. Over and over, the vehicles slammed into each other. Each loud crash sounded like an explosion, driving deeper the truth of Kara's loss. A faint cry rose above the noise of the crash. It didn't sound like it belonged to the scenes playing out before her. It sounded distant and very frightened. She didn't recognize the voice.

Again, the cry for help arose. Kara felt an electric shock as an image of a warehouse flashed before her. The cry was coming from the warehouse. Just as quickly as the image appeared, it was replaced with more automobile accidents.

Kara would get no reprieve from the nightmares until she woke up. Daylight was her only escape, and thankfully for her sake, the sun was beginning to rise.

The next week was a blur for Kara. Funeral arrangements, the funeral itself, and looking for somewhere to live took the majority of her time. Her foster parents' house would be sold at auction. They had no surviving family. Kara had been the only child in their lives, and their careers had kept them so busy that they hadn't updated their wills to include her.

She had 90 days before she had to be out of the house, so the search for a place to live took last place in her list of current priorities. She had gotten through the arrangements with the help of the funeral home staff. She had gotten through the funeral with the help of Yahweh.

She found herself praying to Yahweh more often as the week progressed. Shadow people had been plaguing her more and more, and the scary part was the fact that she was awake.

She saw them at the funeral. They were always just at the edge of her peripheral vision, but they were unmistakable. They were watching her from a distance. She caught glimpses of them when she went out with Blue, and recently, she had begun to see them in her house.

The shadows seemed to vanish when she tried to look directly at them at the funeral. However, the night after the funeral, she had an experience with a shadow that was different.

"I jerked awake from the nightmare, and it was standing over me. I made eye contact and it just stared back with burning hatred in its eyes. I closed my eyes so tight that it hurt and just began to pray. When I opened my eyes again, it was gone."

Kara sat across from Pastor Joshua. She had come by the church early this morning in hopes that Joshua could shed some light on her situation. So much had happened over the last week with the deaths of her foster parents and everything that came with it. She needed this week to be better. It had to get better.

"It sounds like you are under spiritual attack. They are watching you and trying to intimidate you because you have a special call on your life,

Kara." The pastor smiled that warm smile that always made his eyes twinkle.

"It doesn't feel so great." Kara shifted her position in the chair. "Why has Yahweh been silent? It has been over a week, and all I have dreamed about is the crash that killed my foster parents, and that stupid warehouse!"

"The teacher is always silent during the test. I know that sounds cliché, but it is true. Didn't you say the warehouse looked familiar to you?"

"Yes."

"Maybe the Father is trying to tell you something about that. Perhaps that is why it is coming through as a type of interference in your nightmare."

"I suppose that wouldn't be too farfetched. My mind has been pretty cluttered lately." Kara blew a loose strand of hair out of her face.

"It is possible that He is trying to reach you, but the stress of the funeral, and everything you are facing with the supernatural, is making that message difficult to decipher."

The pastor stood up and made his way around the desk to take the chair next to Kara.

"Would you mind if I prayed with you?" Joshua held out his hands for Kara to take.

"Please do. I need some extra help." Kara took his hands and closed her eyes.

Joshua prayed a prayer of peace over Kara. He prayed that her mind would be put at rest and that she be protected from anything that sought to harm her. Finally, he prayed that the meaning of her dream would be made clear to her.

It was a simple prayer, like a conversation with God. It was nothing like the long empty prayers she had heard before. Those prayers had been filled with elegant words and fancy phrases. Not this one though.

She could feel the sincerity of the Pastor, and she realized it wasn't as much about the words as it is the heart of the person praying.

Thanking Joshua for the prayers and support, she made her way out of his office. His next appointment was waiting, and she didn't want to take time away from them.

"Take care. See you Sunday." Joshua said as Kara walked out the door.

"Yes." Looking over her shoulder, Kara replied. "Sunday for sure."

Sunday was still six days away. She just had to get through those six days. She needed to do so many things between now and then, and her sleep-deprived mind wasn't making it easy. She pulled into her driveway and was startled to see Blue running out of the front door to greet her.

The front door of her house was standing open. Kara's pulse quickened as she got out of the car. She knew she had locked the door when she left this morning. Something was wrong.

Kara walked in and immediately choked on the scent of sulfur. Her living room had been ransacked. Furniture was overturned, bookshelves had been stripped of their contents, and their books were tossed haphazardly into a pile.

They were looking for something.

The thought popped into her head, almost as if someone had whispered it to her. She felt the faint presence of Yahweh for a moment, but was quickly overtaken by the harsh realization of what had actually taken place.

She instinctively knew that calling the police would do no good. They weren't equipped to deal with the fiends that had done this. Her house had been ransacked by demons. The acrid scent of sulfur was proof enough of that.

Kara expected to find the same amount of destruction in her room, and probably every other room in the house. She was not disappointed. The entire house had been turned upside down.

"They *were* looking for something." Kara reached down and stroked Blue's head. "I think I know what they were after."

Kara darted back toward the front door and stopped once she reached her car. She took a quick glimpse into the passenger window and saw the brown satchel that held the books given to her by Joshua. Instantly, she realized why she had felt the urge to keep them with her, wherever she went.

They're after the books.

Again, she felt the familiar presence of Yahweh that she had felt in her dreams. Realizing that Yahweh hadn't been as silent as she thought, she retrieved the satchel and walked back into her house to survey the damage.

It was going to take the rest of the day and most of the night to get the mess cleaned up. Kara was determined to return the house to the way it had been just a few hours previously, no matter how long it took, but first she needed food.

"C'mon, boy. Let's see what we can find in the kitchen before we get to work."

Blue cocked his head sideways in response to Kara's voice and loyally followed her into the kitchen.

92

It was nearly three in the morning when Kara had finished getting the house back in order. She sighed as she looked in the bathroom mirror, if you could call it that. Only one shard of glass survived the assault on her home, but it was at least big enough to show her the dark circles under her eyes and the dirt smeared across her face.

She needed a shower, but it would wait until she woke up. She prioritized sleep over feeling clean, and fell into bed still wearing the clothes she'd put on that morning.

It wasn't very long after closing her eyes that she found herself in a familiar setting. For the first time in over a week she was not seeing car crashes, but instead the mist and dark path of her recurring dream about Yahweh and Azazel was back.

Only, it wasn't a dream. She had learned that her experiences here were just as real as her experiences in the waking world. Yahweh had called it a spirit realm. This time there was no black gate or blinding light. There was only the path ahead of her.

She could feel the presence of evil. It was a feeling that she had grown accustomed to over the last couple of weeks. A feeling that haunted her even when she was awake. The faint smell of sulfur was carried by a breeze that whipped strands of her hair back into her face.

She pulled her hair into a high ponytail using the hair tie that she wore as a bracelet, and began to walk forward along the path. The feeling of being watched intensified the more she walked, and she thought she saw dark forms moving in the mist.

Anticipating trouble, Kara willed her armor into place. The ebony platemail encrusted with amethyst crystals as fasteners appeared on her body. She reached behind her back and drew her sword, creating a high-pitched metallic ring as the blade released from its sheath.

Kara moved forward, step-by-step, with her weapon at the ready. She scanned the mist for moving objects, but was unable to detect anything visibly. However, the prickle on the back of her neck let her know they were there. It was only a matter of time before they struck.

She approached a split in the path. The path to her left seemed the safer of the two choices. It was brightly lit, and the mist seemed to dissipate. The one to the right led downward, and seemed less safe with all of the twists and turns amidst the heavy mist clinging to the path.

Just as Kara was about to take the left-hand path, she heard a cry for help coming from her right.

She squinted down the path and could make out the faint shape of a warehouse building. At that moment, she knew which path she had to take and tightened the grip on her sword. Just a few paces down the right-hand path revealed more of the landscape and she could see the warehouse more clearly.

She wound down the path, navigating the twists and turns with care, but had yet to be attacked by the creatures hidden within the mist. As she grew closer to the warehouse, the path transitioned into pavement.

Kara noticed streetlights illuminating the street ahead of her. Businesses lined the sides, and cars were parked out front. She recognized some of the shops and realized that she was walking down the streets of her hometown, or at least a version of it.

Dark shapes moved just out of sight. She thought she saw something dart behind a box van parked in front of a mom-and-pop pharmacy at the end of the block. The warehouse that the cry was coming from sat one street over.

That meant she would have to pass the box truck that she was fairly certain concealed a shadow demon waiting to pounce. She crept closer to the van, keeping a watchful eye for surprise attacks. With her back against the back of the truck, she readied her sword and jumped around to the side of the van ready to strike.

Nothing was there aside from the faint scent of sulfur. "Okay Kara, you're letting your imagination get the best of you." She may have actually believed the words she told herself, had she not experienced all that she had over the last few weeks. As it were, the words that were meant to ease her nerves brought no comfort.

She was one street away from the warehouse, and the faint cry she originally heard had become louder. The amount of sorrow in the cry was enough to bring tears to her eyes. Whoever it was, they were desperate.

"Help! Please, someone save us! Please God!"

Kara was urged forward from the sheer desperation in the cry from the unknown girl. Before she realized it, she was standing just outside the parking lot of the warehouse. The rusty chain link gate was closed to prevent access to the building.

She wasn't getting into the warehouse without climbing the fence, and she would have done so if it wasn't for the ten-foot-tall shadow demon she saw guarding the main door to the building. It was at that moment Kara realized that, while she had been distracted by the girl's cries, her unseen watchers had arrived and were closing in on her from behind.

She swung around and caught her closest assailant with a glancing blow to its shoulder. Something like black smoke escaped from the wound. It staggered back a few paces, allowing Kara to rush through the open spot in the ranks of shadow creatures closing in on her.

There had to be at least six of them. They weren't ten feet tall like the thing guarding the warehouse, but they were still bigger than her in every way. Yellow eyes burned like embers from the solid black heads of the creatures.

A few of them had features that resembled men. However, when the one Kara had cut opened its mouth in a scream filled with rage, she saw long fangs in place of human incisors. She finished it off by driving her sword into its chest. The creature vanished in a plume of black smoke, leaving behind the scent of sulfur that gagged Kara and made it difficult to breathe.

She ran several paces away from her assailants in an attempt to fill her lungs with fresh air. It was an added bonus that it put some distance between her and the demons pursuing her. Kara stopped short before slamming into the twisted black gate that had blocked her path in previous dreams, if she could even call them dreams anymore. At least she could breathe again, for now. The demons were only a few yards away.

She had to escape. There were too many for her to fight off. In an attempt to climb the gate, she grabbed the twisted iron, ready to pull herself over, but jerked her hand away as searing pain shot through her hand and up her arm. The metal was so cold that it burned. She looked at her palm and saw the long black burn seared into her flesh. She was left with no choice but to fight. So, she would fight.

Kara decided to bring the fight to them. She charged straight ahead with her sight set on the demon closest to her. It was smaller than some of the others in height, but made up for it in mass. She knew that if this brute got a hold of her, she would be crushed to death in an instant.

Just a few paces away from colliding with the musclebound demon, Kara jumped into the air and flipped forward, bringing her sword down in an arc that split the demon's head in half. When she landed, she kept running toward the other demons to avoid getting trapped in the fog of sulfur the brute would leave behind.

The demons were brandishing weapons of their own. The one closest to her swung a morning star with such fury that Kara felt the wind from the massive steel ball covered with sharp spikes as it narrowly missed her head. She struck her assailant just under its attacking arm, and plunged her sword deep. She intended to pierce its heart, assuming that it had one.

Heart or no heart, she had dispatched another attacker. The cloud of sulfur fumed out in all directions like a ripple in a lake. Kara pushed herself harder to stay ahead of it. Three down and too many to go. Kara felt her strength beginning to wane. She had to press on. She didn't want to think about the nagging question in the back of her mind.

If I die in this dream, or spirit world, or wherever I am...will I die in the real world?

She hurled herself forward into a slide only a few paces away from a demon that held a massive spear. She slid between its legs and brought her sword up in a devastating arc that split the demon down the middle, much like she had split the head of her first attacker. Only, this time, she wasn't fast enough to avoid the acrid sulfur that infiltrated her lungs and took her vision.

She could hear her attackers closing in on her, and got the feeling she was about to get the answer to that troublesome question about death. She saw a blurry shape lunging toward her with what she assumed was a dangerously sharp weapon aimed at her chest.

Kara managed to dodge the attack but was unable to counter before the next attacker was on her. Searing pain in her left thigh let her know she had been hit. What had hit her, though, was a mystery. Her sight was badly impaired from the thick, sulfurous fog that hung in the air.

A blast of wind knocked Kara off her feet and blew her several feet backward. However, it managed to clear the air enough for her to breathe and she was able to make out a figure standing in the distance. The figure was barely a silhouette, but the massive set of wings were clearly visible, and they emanated a bright, white light and sent strong gusts of wind with each flap.

Her remaining attackers lay scattered around her, blown over by the force of those wings. As her sight returned to her, she saw her apparent rescuer more clearly. His wings were now still, and he appeared to be made from light that was housed in the likeness of a large human male.

"They won't be down for long. If you hope to survive this, run to me. With everything you have left, run!"

Kara felt the words more than she heard them. It was like they had been spoken directly into her mind, or more to her spirit. She could only assume this guy played for the opposite team than that of the demons, so she ran.

She pushed her body beyond normal physical limits and ran toward the light until the light was so bright it consumed her, and she couldn't see anything else.

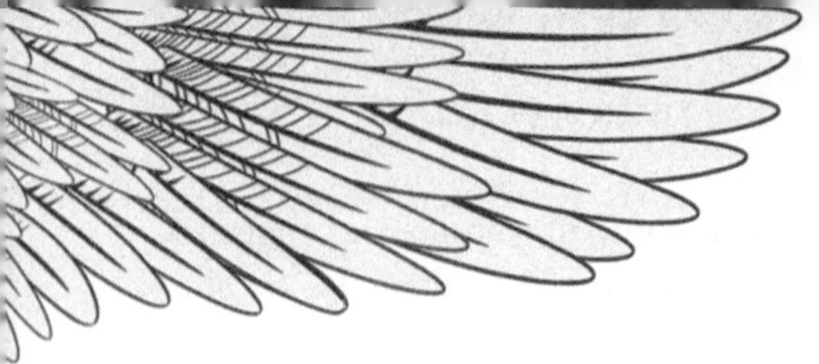

Kara squinted as the sun shone in through the window opposite of her bed. She had forgotten to close the blinds before she'd collapsed from exhaustion only a few hours earlier.

The last thing she remembered was running toward a massive, white-winged angel. At least, what she'd *thought* was an angel. However, unlike Azazel, this one was a good angel. The bright light coming from this one had enveloped her, blinding her while also bathing her in complete joy and peace.

He had rescued her from certain death. She was sure of that. Happy to be alive, Kara said a short prayer of gratitude to Yahweh for sending one of his warriors to her rescue. Rubbing the sleep out of her eyes, she got out of bed and headed for the shower.

⸻ ✦✦✦ ⸻

Fresh from the shower, Kara slipped on some jeans, a fitted black shirt, and her sneakers. She scratched Blue behind his ears on her way out of the front door, not even stopping to grab a breakfast bar. She wanted to take a drive to where she thought the warehouse was that she had dreamed about earlier. She desperately needed answers.

It was a beautiful day for a drive, she just wished she had a better destination. It still felt odd for the rest of the world to appear so normal, while her world became stranger each day. Her world was getting tricky to navigate, and it seemed that the lines were beginning to blur from the waking world and wherever it was that she went when she dreamed.

This is definitely the place.

Kara put her car in park a few feet away from a locked gate guarding what appeared to be an abandoned warehouse. There was a weathered sign on the gate indicating that the property had been condemned by the city, and from the looks of it, it had been condemned years ago.

If this place is condemned, whose vehicle is that back there?

A white box van caught Kara's eye, and she got out to investigate. She had no idea what she would do once she was out of the car, but she wanted a closer look.

"Stop!"

The gruff voice caught Kara off guard. She wasn't going to get a closer look, at least not right now. A man approached her from the left. He was wearing black cargo pants, a dark grey spandex shirt under a black tactical vest, and military style boots. The sun glinted off the barrel of the assault rifle slung across his shoulder as he approached.

"You're not supposed to be here."

"I'm sorry. I didn't mean to cause any trouble. I just got out to stretch my legs." Kara felt heat spread across her cheeks. She hadn't counted on anyone being here.

"It's fine. You need to leave, though. The building is off limits." His mouth was set and the muscles in his jaw rippled as he bit down on the toothpick hanging out of his mouth.

"Why is that exactly?" Kara was shocked at herself for asking.

"It's condemned. It's dangerous. What is your business here?" He took a step forward, closer to Kara.

"Like I said, I just got out to stretch my legs and thought I saw something in the parking lot. I just wanted a closer look."

"What was it that you thought you saw, exactly?" Kara felt her resolve begin to fade under his scrutiny.

"I...I'm not sure, exactly. Something just caught the corner of my eye."

The man with the gun just stared at her. She was beginning to get extremely uncomfortable, and took a few steps back in the direction of her vehicle.

"Officer, I'll leave." Her voice trembled as she spoke but she found herself asking another surprising question. "It *is* Officer, isn't it?"

"No. I work for a private security firm, and my employer was very clear about not letting anyone near this property." He lowered his aviator sunglasses and locked his steel blue gaze directly onto Kara. "I'm just doing my job. Now, beat it."

Kara turned and got back in her car. Her engine roared to life, and she pulled off as quickly as she could. The nausea that Kara felt when he locked his eyes onto her was awfully familiar. She had felt it before, in her dreams when evil was near. However, she was wide awake, and that feeling scared her far worse now that she couldn't armor up.

As Kara drove back to her house, she couldn't stop thinking about the warehouse. Now she knew there was something there she needed to see. She just needed to figure out how to get past the creepy guard.

She pulled into her driveway and noticed a piece of paper had been taped to her door. Once she got to the door, she saw she had been mistaken.

The paper hadn't been taped to her door. It had been *pinned* to her door, with a knife. The dark steel blade was wicked looking and reminded her of something from *Lord of the Rings*.

The note, however, chilled her blood. Scribbled on the paper were the words, "Stay away from the warehouse. You've been warned." She grasped the bone handle and yanked the blade free from the door. She walked into her house with the note in one hand and the knife in the other.

Stay away? Yeah, no chance of that. I'm going back—tonight!

Shadows gathered in the corner of the abandoned warehouse. A meeting had been called, and Azazel was coming to address his cohort. The temperature dropped in the room when the fallen angel arrived.

"Master, she was here." The security guard's gravelly voice croaked out—or, rather, the voice of the spirit inhabiting him did.

"I'm aware. She'll be back tonight. She has a bad habit of talking to herself. We were listening."

"Do you want me to have this," he motioned toward the body of the guard he inhabited, "here tonight? Scare her away?"

"That won't be necessary. In fact, I want you to ditch the meat puppet. By tonight, you won't need him any longer. Tonight, you will once again be able to roam the earth in whatever form you wish to take." Azazel paused and looked directly up at the girls hanging in the cages.

"The days of needing these *humans* to get around and accomplish our plans are at an end."

The guard's body crumpled to the ground as black fog poured out from his mouth. Towering over the corpse on the ground stood a ten-foot-tall shadow.

"Yes, master. I'll take care of her tonight. She'll never get the chance to become the warrior that she's supposed to be." The demon motioned over his shoulder to the three other shadow beings in the corner.

"She thinned our ranks on her latest dream walk. We almost had her, and then *Yahweh* interfered." He spat the name out.

"Deal with her tonight. Make an example out of her. Show good ol' *dad* that we're done playing by the rules. She'll be in the physical world, so she'll be vulnerable."

Azazel vanished in a flash of blinding red light. The shadow demon had a wicked grin spreading across his face. The things he would do to this girl brought him much joy, and would bring her a great deal of suffering, and eventually—death.

The girls in the cages, the few that were still moving, watched as their captor appeared to be talking to himself in a dark corner of the warehouse.

The air filled with a horrible smell that burned their eyes and nostrils. They watched as their captor fell to the floor, convulsed a few times, and became still.

This was either incredibly good for them, or very bad. The girl who had been praying hoped that it was good but was concerned about how they would ever get out of there when the only person who knew where they were had just dropped dead.

She closed her eyes and wept. Then she prayed, and then she wept again. Tears stained her face as she cried herself to sleep, unaware of the intense yellow eyes watching her from the corner.

She would be the first one they killed when they became corporeal again. They desperately wanted to silence her prayers.

16

Kara looked down at the knife that she had in her hand. It looked ancient. The dark metal almost looked black, but had a subtle red shimmer to it. Runes had been carved into the blade, and the handle looked like bone.

"What do ya think, boy?"

Blue cocked his head sideways and looked at Kara. He sniffed the blade and tucked his tail between his legs and ran off to find his kennel. Whatever it was, he did not like it, and Kara wasn't so sure that she did, either. It felt strange. It was too light in her hand for its size, and it felt warm to the touch.

She really wanted more information about this blade. After all, someone or *something* had stabbed it into her door. She was leaning toward the latter. Then it dawned on her. Pastor Joshua may know something about it.

Kara slipped her shoes on and ran out of the door to get in her car. The knife was tucked away safely in her console. She would ask the pastor about it before she carried it into the church. It felt wrong to bring whatever it was into a sacred place.

Kara stopped her car abruptly as she approached the church. Her stomach sank as she saw the flames erupting from the roof. The area had been blocked off with police cars as firetrucks sprayed the building with multiple hoses. The water did little to abate the flames.

Kara could feel the heat as she got out of her car and began to make her way toward the church. She spotted Tommy standing on the other side of the police line and quickened her pace to reach him.

Stopping short of the barricade, she called out to Tommy, hoping that he could hear her over the roar of the fire. He finally turned his head in her direction, and Kara knew that something was wrong. It was evident he was distraught as he jogged over to her.

"Tommy, what happened?"

"I have no idea. Pastor Joshua sent me out to get lunch and I came back to...THIS!" He waved his hands in the direction of the burning church.

"Did Pastor Joshua make it out?" Kara tried to swallow around the lump in her throat.

"I, I don't think so. Him and his wife were inside. I overheard the firemen saying they heard someone in there but couldn't get in due to structural integrity issues. One of them tried and was ordered back by the captain. He said the fire was too hot, hotter than it should be, and that the building was collapsing too fast." Tommy swiped away a tear, smearing soot on his face.

"This is unbelievable. I just talked to him yesterday. This can't be happening." Kara was crying.

Tommy put an arm around her shoulders in a feeble attempt to offer comfort, and they cried together as they watched their church burn to the ground with some of the most kind people she had ever known still inside.

⸺·⟨◆◆⟩·⸻

Kara would mourn later. Now, more than ever, she was determined to get back to the warehouse when the sun went down. She had a few hours to prepare and decided that she needed to eat something, even though she didn't feel like it. She would need her strength to get through what the night would hold.

She let the dagger fall to the bed, along with her bag. First, she had to get the soot and the smell from the fire off of her as quickly as possible. She peeled off her clothes and went to the bathroom for a shower.

It reminded her too much of the smell the demons left behind after being dispatched to wherever dead demons go. She felt that she was responsible for the fire at the church, and she couldn't shake the guilt that threatened to paralyze her.

She kept telling herself that if she had never gone to Joshua, he and his wife would still be alive. One thing she knew for sure. The next time she dreamed, she was going to make them pay.

Until then, she needed to find out what was going on at the warehouse. She dried off quickly and slipped on a pair of black pants and a black long-sleeved shirt. The idea was to not be seen this time around.

Kara went into the kitchen to make a sandwich for herself, and saw Blue staring at his empty food bowl.

"Sorry, boy." She scratched behind his ears and filled his bowl before making her sandwich.

Kara sat down at the dining table and opened her laptop. She searched for information on the dagger while she ate. After scrolling through what seemed like endless pages of search results, she found a picture of the dagger with a link to a website.

She clicked the link and was met with heavy metal music. The noise coming from the speakers was horrible, but the imagery on her screen was worse. She had stumbled onto a satanic website that wasn't shy about the fact that they sacrificed animals.

She found the picture of the dagger close to the bottom of the page. The article claimed that it was the weapon of a demon. It went on to say that someone named "Matthias Shand" had successfully summoned a demon, and that the dagger was given to him as a gift. The only catch was that he had to spill the blood of an innocent every new moon.

It said that the dagger had been taken by police when Matthias was arrested for attempting to murder a three-year-old child two years ago. The article went on to lament the loss of the demonic gift.

Kara clicked the back button on her browser and did a search for "Matthias Shand". The first search result confirmed what the sketchy website had claimed. Matthias had been arrested, and a ceremonial weapon had been taken from him at the scene.

Kara closed her laptop and put her plate in the sink. She went to her room and retrieved the dagger from the bed. Turning the dagger over in her hand, she examined each rune that was etched into the blade. It certainly felt like it could be a dagger with supernatural properties.

Is this the real deal? Did this belong to a demon?

So many thoughts ran through her head, it was hard to keep track. The only thing she knew for sure was that it felt lighter than it should be, given its size, and it was warm to the touch. It also seemed to vibrate. It was such a fast vibration, that it was almost unnoticeable, but she could feel it.

She laid it down beside her as she slipped on her black boots and laced them up. She stood and went to the mirror. She tied back her dark hair into a high ponytail and slipped it through the opening in the back of a black ball cap.

She glanced at herself one last time in the mirror. Seeing the broken mirror caused a rush of grief as she thought about her own brokenness and the loss of her foster parents and Pastor Joshua. She shook her head to bring her thoughts back to the present.

She was all blacked out except for her hands and face. If she had owned black gloves, she would have worn them. However, a black ski mask was where she drew the line. She didn't want to get mistaken for a criminal and get herself shot.

She grabbed her keys and went for the door, but stopped short. As a last-minute thought, she grabbed a shirt out of her closet and wrapped the blade in it. She tucked the weapon into the waistband of her pants. The bone handle was warm against the small of her back, but made her skin prickle as if it were cold.

Kara pulled her shirt down over the handle of the weapon in an attempt at concealment. She opened the front door and turned back to Blue who had taken up his position at the door to see her off.

"You be good, Blue. I'll be back. I hope."

Kara brought her car to a stop a block away from the warehouse this time. She wanted to scout the area first and make sure tall, dark, and creepy wasn't patrolling the area. She wondered if he would still have the sunglasses on at night to hide his unsettling eyes.

She scanned the streets and nearby parking areas. There was no sign of anyone. Everything felt eerily quiet, which probably wasn't a good sign. She watched the warehouse intently. The white box van was still parked in the back of the parking lot.

Aside from the tarp that partially covered the van blowing in the wind, there was no movement. No lights on in the parking lot, no lights on in the warehouse, everything looked abandoned. The only source of light was the dim bulbs of the streetlights, and the small flashlight she had brought to use once she got closer.

She sat for what seemed like an eternity. Glancing at the clock in her car, she saw that it was almost midnight. She whispered a quick prayer to Yahweh asking for guidance.

"If this is what you have been trying to show me, please help me to see it though. Keep me safe, please. Thanks? Amen?" Kara looked to the sky apologetically.

She was still learning how to be a Christian, and prayer wasn't always easy. Giving her surroundings a final scan, she stepped out of her car and eased the door closed as silently as she could. She stood in perfect silence—the insects didn't even make a sound.

Eerie!

Kara crept toward the warehouse making sure that she kept to the shadows. She couldn't afford to be seen by anyone before she found out what was going on in this warehouse.

The gate was shut with a padlock in place on the rusty chain. So far, there had been no sign of the security guard she ran into earlier, but she still wasn't getting in through the gate and the fence was too high for her to scale, if she was being honest with herself.

"Walk around the fence. There's an opening on the right side, about halfway down."

Kara recognized the subtle voice speaking to her spirit, and she obeyed. She was getting further away from the streetlights and clicked on her flashlight. Careful to get the beam angled to the ground, she tried to minimize the spread of light with her free hand. Kara found the opening in the fence and stooped down to go through it.

Kara stood frozen inside the fence. She took time to do another scan of her surroundings. She appeared to still be alone, but the hair on the back of her neck was standing up and she felt a familiar wave of nausea wash over her. She had unseen company.

Two pairs of yellow eyes followed every move that Kara made. The unseen beings that walked right behind Kara were flickering in and out of existence. Whatever it was that would allow them to take their physical forms was beginning to transpire. It was not complete though, or Kara would already be dead.

The shadow demons kept pace with her, waiting for the opportunity to strike. Kara got closer to the doors of the warehouse and picked up another unseen stalker. One of the demons went back inside to report to his master.

"Good. Let her come." A sinister smile spread across the face of the ten-foot-tall demon that oversaw this particular operation.

The smaller demon took his perch next to the suspended cages with the girls. The praying girl whimpered slightly as she moved her lips in prayer. She felt her life draining from her body, and knew this would probably be the last prayer she would be able to pray.

The demon perched next to her mocked her in silence and awaited his opportunity to choke the life from this pitiful waif of a human.

<hr>

Kara tried the handle of the front door. It was secured. She wasn't gaining entry to the warehouse through the main door. She had seen a side door on the side of the building when she approached.

Kara made her way around the building intent on finding the side door. The faint sound of a woman crying stopped her about ten paces short of the door. She craned her neck to see a window that had been broken. It was entirely too high for her to see into, so she did the only thing she knew to do and tried the door.

The handle squeaked in protest as it slowly turned. Kara put her weight against the door and it inched open. She stepped inside the warehouse and waited a moment for her eyes to adjust to the pitch black that greeted her.

The soft crying was coming from the back of the warehouse. Once her eyes had adjusted, Kara aimed her flashlight just a few inches in front of her feet and crept forward, exercising an abundance of caution.

Large equipment lined the walls on both sides of her. She kept to the shadows cast by the equipment and kept her focus on the small roll up door at the back of the building. That was where she heard the cry from and that was where she was headed.

The deeper she ventured into the building; the smell of rust and must was replaced with an acrid odor that turned her stomach. The scent of sulfur and human excrement hung heavily in the air. She covered her nose with her free hand, but it did little to stop the assault on her senses. It was a tangible odor that she could almost taste.

Tightening down on her resolve, Kara pressed forward. The closer she got to the door, the stronger the odor, as well as her urge to vomit, became. Kara turned off her flashlight just before walking through the door. There was enough ambient light to see in this new space, and what she saw made her blood run cold.

Kara's body went rigid at the scene before her. It was too much to process at first. Slowly, different elements began to come into focus. The body of the security guard lay crumpled on the floor.

Dark holes, where his eyes should have been, stared up at her. His mouth was contorted into an expression of sheer terror and something black dripped from it, forming a pool on the floor beneath him. The ashen gray color of his skin told her that he had been dead for several hours.

A weak cry for help broke her away from the horrific scene before her.

"Help! Up here!"

Kara looked up to her right to see a rusty cage hanging from the ceiling. It was one of several cages, and each cage had a young girl inside. The only girl who was moving was calling to her for help.

"Please. Get me out of here!" The girl begged through cracked and bleeding lips.

Kara was shocked at the condition the girl was in. She was skin and bones, and about three shades whiter than Kara's bed sheets. Dark circles ringed her eyes, and her fingernails were bloody stumps from multiple attempts at getting out of her cage. She had been stripped down to her underwear, and, from the looks of it, badly beaten.

Kara was looking at someone on the brink of death, and she had no clue what to do next. She had to get her down. She had to get her some help. Kara reached into her pocket to retrieve her cell phone, when her heart sank. In her haste to leave, she had left her phone on the counter.

"Hang on, okay? I'm going to figure something out. Just stay with me." Kara tried to put conviction into her trembling voice as she looked around for something to use.

Kara tried to remain calm as she searched for a solution to get this girl out of the cage. She traced the chain holding the cage to a gear box on the ceiling. That gear box had a long cord hanging from it with a remote attached to the end. The red and green buttons on the remote lit up like a beacon to Kara.

She raced over to the remote, no longer concerned with stealth, and pressed the green button. The cage began to lift higher.

No! That's not what I need!

Kara pressed the red button and the cage jolted to a stop, causing the girl inside to cry out as she was knocked back to the floor of her prison.

"I'm so sorry," Kara said with tears in her eyes. "Let me try again."

Kara searched the remote and found a switch on the side that had up and down arrows. She pressed the down arrow clicking it into place. Kara pressed the green button, and this time the cage began a slow decent as the low rumble of the gear box kicked in.

"I'm getting you out of…"

Kara's words were cut short as she felt a vice-like grip on both of her arms. She was being pulled back away from the cage and found herself suspended four feet off of the ground. The searing pain radiating from the impossibly tight grip on each wrist made her vision blurry at the edges.

The girl inside the cage screamed the most raw and horrified sound that Kara had ever heard.

18

The girl in the cage watched in terror as her rescuer was violently jerked back from the cage and lifted into the air by an unseen force. She saw bruises begin to form on her wrists as she hung in the air with her arms outstretched, unable to move.

The caged girl couldn't hold in a scream of terror as she saw two shadow beings begin to materialize. There was one on each side of the girl who had tried to help her, holding her by the wrists. Their yellow eyes blinked in and out of existence several times before they became fully visible.

She had never seen anything like this in her short life, and was certain she wouldn't live past today to ever see anything like it again. They were the tallest creatures she had ever seen, standing at just over eight feet tall. She shrank back when a third set of eyes appeared. They had to belong to something even larger than these two, something ten feet or taller.

The eyes appeared behind the girl being held by these creatures, and, as this new arrival made his way out of the shadows, the girl in the cage fainted.

<hr>

Kara struggled against her unseen captors, but there was no escaping their iron grasp. Her heart banged against her ribs at an alarming rate that only increased as her assailants begin to flicker in and out of sight.

Kara willed her armor into place, but nothing happened. Desperate, Kara tried again, and, when that failed, she tried again. Still, nothing happened.

I'm awake. No armor in the waking world. This is it. This is how I die.

Her thoughts ran through her mind like a freight train. However, they came crashing to a halt when Kara felt the room shake as an immense presence emerged from the shadows behind her. Each step that brought him closer to her caused debris to fall from the ceiling beams.

The giant demon came around Kara from the left and stood directly in front of her. Even though she was lifted off of the ground, she still had to raise her head to see his yellow eyes burning into hers. This was the same massive demon that had guarded the warehouse in her last dream, only *this* was no dream.

"Yahweh! Please help me!"

The demon winced at the name, but recovered quickly and let out a laugh that left Kara wishing she could cover her ears.

"Pathetic human! Your god cannot save you. Do you not know who it is that stands before you?" The demon jeered at her.

She took in his form—although it was still flickering in and out of reality, she could make out details that hadn't been present during any of the other interactions that she'd had with the creature.

Scaled armor shimmered across his chest and thighs. A thick beard adorned his face, and, as she brought her gaze up, she noticed the gaping wound in the center of his forehead and the cracked fragments of helmet that were embedded in the wound.

Kara remembered something from the book of Enoch that had said that demons were the disembodied spirits of the dead Nephilim, the giants of old. She knew who it was that stood before her.

"Goliath."

"Goliath of Gath! Watch your god-licking tongue and tremble before me!" His voice threatened to deafen Kara.

His form was gaining more solidity, and the flickering was becoming less frequent. The way Kara figured, she only had minutes before he could cause her some serious harm.

"*I may not be able to harm you here, but a time is coming when this world and your waking world will begin to merge, and then I will destroy you as I have promised.*" The words of Azazel rang fresh in her mind.

She was witnessing that merger take place, right now, and she was helpless to do anything but watch. The only thing she had going for her was that this wasn't Azazel standing in front of her, or she would most likely be dead already.

Looking to her right and to her left, Kara knew she wasn't breaking free from the grips of the fanged creatures holding her. They reminded her of vampires, but bigger than the movies made them out to be. She had no way of fighting Goliath aside from her words, so she would use those.

"Tremble? Are you serious?" Kara mocked.

Goliath snapped his head and his eyes shrunk down to pinpricks of bright amber. This was the response that Kara had hoped for. She would use his vanity against him—she hoped.

"I've read about you. You thought highly of yourself all those thousands of years ago. How did that work out for you?" Kara worked ridiculously hard to hide the fear from her voice.

"I'll kill you!" Goliath brought his face so close to hers that his breath blew her hair back.

"Like you planned on killing David? Ha! I think we *know* how that worked out, right? That nasty hole in your head seems like the perfect answer to my question." Kara sent up a silent prayer.

Yahweh, please protect me. Don't let me die like this, please.

"Weren't you, like, the smallest giant ever?"

Kara knew she was close to his breaking point and that he was close to being fully materialized into her realm. If he didn't snap soon, her plan may just kill her.

Goliath fumed and clenched his fists tight at his side. His eyes glowed violently, and a sulfuric fog escaped his mouth as he spoke.

"I will destroy you—slowly. You will know suffering before death and there is nothing that your god can do to stop me. This is our domain, given to us *legally*, millennia ago. You have no idea what you have brought upon yourself, meddling in the affairs of Azazel." Goliath wiped the fog-like substance from his mouth. "I will erase you from the earth!"

Kara sent up one last silent plea for aid and then triggered her trap, hoping that it wasn't too late.

"Then, do it…*little* man."

Kara felt the air forced from her lungs by the explosive impact that hit her directly in the chest. She felt it as the grip of the fanged creatures broke free, and she felt herself travel several feet back and away from her attacker.

Her plan had worked perfectly—and also failed miserably. She had been knocked free and given the distance to escape and return later with authorities to free the girl. However, the blow had done much more damage than she had anticipated, and she was unable to move as darkness clouded her vision. She heard the ring of steel hitting the concrete floor and realized that her concealed dagger had been knocked free as a result of the concussive punch.

The dagger was inches from her hand, but she didn't have the strength to move. Goliath spotted it immediately and roared in rage.

"What are you doing with that?! That isn't for filthy human hands!"

Kara wanted to say that she supposed his messenger got sloppy, but she was unable to move her mouth. She watched as Goliath started moving towards the dagger, and anticipated the searing pain of it tearing into her flesh. She gave out before he was halfway to her and slipped into the blackness that had been threatening to invade her vision.

Kara's head rolled from one side to the other as she tried to get her bearings. She opened her eyes and was nearly blinded by the bright light that shone before her.

"Am I dead?"

"No, my child—just unconscious. You need to wake up, though. You don't want to miss an answered prayer, do you?"

"Yahweh?"

"Awaken!"

Kara's eyes fluttered open in the waking world, and she realized that she must have only been out for a split second. Goliath was still making his way towards her when a loud crash from the front of the warehouse made him pause.

She took advantage of this momentary distraction and grabbed the dagger while he was barking orders to the other two demons. She hid the dagger under her body.

"You, go check that out. I don't want anyone interfering with what I have planned for this one." Goliath nodded toward Kara.

The demon scurried off toward the front of the warehouse, and, only seconds later, another loud crash was heard as the demon was hurled through the wall next to the roll up door.

"Oops. Looks like I missed the door."

The voice belonged to a girl, not much older than Kara. She stepped into the room and unsheathed a sword from her back. The room grew brighter from the light emanating from the sword, and Kara was able to get a good look at her.

She appeared to be human, with brunette hair pulled into a high braid that cascaded midway down her back. She was wearing leather, and lots of it. She wore black leather pants, and a black leather top that resembled an armored vest. She wore a fitted white t-shirt beneath the vest, and leather wrist guards on each arm.

A black biker boot smashed into the face of the demon that had come through the wall, and then the new girl brought her sword down, severing the demon's head from its body.

"One down and two to go. I was expecting more."

In response to the taunt, five more gruesome demons materialized behind Goliath.

"Ah, that's more like it."

"You're not supposed to be here!" Goliath was furious. "This isn't your territory!"

"I go where I'm instructed, filthy demon."

"Kill her!" Goliath roared.

The newcomer went into action, and Kara could do nothing but watch in amazement as she spun and dashed around the demons, slashing and hacking in the most graceful dance of death that Kara had ever seen. It was like watching a scene from a movie.

Three of the five demons were down before Kara could really get a grasp of what was happening. The remaining two charged the new girl with lightning speed. One dashed at her from the ground, and the other leaped into the air in an attempted strike from above.

In one fluid motion, the unknown girl retrieved two small daggers from her arm guards and flung them simultaneously at her attackers. Both demons vanished into a puff of black smoke as the blades made contact with their bodies, and left the room stinking of sulfur.

"Well, that just leaves me and you. Goliath, I presume? I thought you'd be bigger."

Who IS this girl? Kara's mind raced as she watched the scene before her. She was beginning to feel her strength return, but had no intention of running away now.

"I thought the same of you, guardian." He spoke with a sense of familiarity. "Very well, I suppose this day brings many disappointments." Goliath held out his hand and an immense spear materialized. "It doesn't matter, you'll be dead soon enough."

Kara watched in wonder as the two fought one another. Goliath stabbed his spear forward with unexpected speed, and the new girl side stepped and countered almost effortlessly. This back and forth went on for what seemed like an eternity to Kara.

Slowly, as she watched the battle taking place only a few feet away from her, Kara pulled herself into a sitting position and dragged herself further away from the action. She hid behind a stack of metal containers and continued observing the confrontation.

The girl rolled under Goliath's legs and slashed his Achilles tendon with her return swing. Black fog poured from the wound as Goliath stumbled to his knees. He fought to stay upright and lunged at his opponent with a vicious spear strike. She barely dodged in time to avoid being impaled, and instead got the top of her shoulder slashed for her trouble.

Bright red blood trickled down her arm, and she winced in pain as she spun away from the blade of the spear and brought her own weapon in for an attack.

"You're bleeding, pitiful human!" Goliath's face was overtaken by a demonic grin.

"So are you." The new girl thrust her sword forward with a grunt. "Now, you're done!"

She drove her blade deep into the chest of Goliath, only stopping when the hilt was flush against his chest. Goliath's grin turned into an expression of shock, and then he slumped forward, leaking black fog that covered the area around him.

The newcomer turned to face Kara—not realizing that her enemy was down, but not out.

"Look out!" Kara screamed with everything she had left in her, but her warning was too late.

Goliath had swept the legs of the girl out from under her with the butt-end of his spear and was on her before she landed. She was able to get her sword up in time to block what would have been a fatal attack and the spear clattered to the floor.

Enraged, Goliath used what weapons he had left. He opened his mouth impossibly wide, revealing two rows of teeth. The back row was lined with sharp tips and two extra-long canine teeth on top and bottom. If he couldn't take her head with his spear, he would bite it off and drain her dry when he was finished.

Goliath reared back and his jaw appeared to dislocate, allowing his mouth to open unnaturally large, and he dove down into the fog toward the new girl's throat.

Kara sprang into action.

The wind from his strike blew the fog away enough that Kara was able to see that the girl had gotten the blade of her sword between her throat and Goliath's mouth. It was evident that her strength was fading, though.

Kara sped forward with the dagger grasped in her hand. Goliath was biting at the blade and struggling to get the sword out of the girl's hands with his only good arm. His other arm had been severed during the battle. In fact, he had been so injured that Kara was shocked he was still able to fight.

The other demons had been dispatched by the unknown warrior's weapons upon a killing blow. Goliath was different in some way. He was injured by them, but didn't appear to be able to be destroyed in the same way as the others had.

Kara had closed the distance and was standing directly behind Goliath. She bit down on the pain in her body and managed some parting words to the giant demon.

"You wanted this thing so bad. Here, take it!" Kara growled out the last words and thrust the demonic dagger deep into Goliath's back.

The other girl felt the weight that was pressing on her release. She saw the tip of a twisted blade erupt through the chest of the raging demon on top of her. Goliath disintegrated into a shower of red-hot embers and a cloud of sulfuric black smoke, and she saw the face of Kara staring down at her.

The blade shook in Kara's white-knuckled grip, and sweat was dripping from her forehead.

"You okay?" Kara asked.

"I am. I was about to ask you the same question."

Kara gave a weak smile and collapsed onto the floor next to the unknown warrior who had undoubtedly saved her from certain death.

I guess I kinda saved her too.

That was Kara's last thought before she lost consciousness.

When Kara's eyes opened again, they were flooded with red and blue flashing lights. She was a block away from the warehouse, propped up against a dumpster. Police cars and ambulances filled the parking lot of the warehouse. There was a firetruck parked outside of the gate, spraying water on her burning car.

"They had no intention of giving you a way of escape."

Kara looked to her right and saw her rescuer sitting beside her with her back propped against the dumpster. She had torn off a piece of her t-shirt and bandaged the wound on her shoulder.

Kara looked back at the warehouse and saw bodies covered with sheets lined up outside the building.

"No, I was too late."

"Not for everyone. We saved a few tonight. You did good."

Kara saw the girl, who was in the cage she had lowered, wrapped in a blanket and sitting in the back of an ambulance. There were two other girls, each in a different ambulance. They would survive thanks to her efforts and those of her unknown friend.

Kara looked back to her right, but the girl was gone. She stood up and looked around frantically. She hadn't even got a chance to thank her for what she had done.

"Did you lose something?"

Kara spun around and saw the other girl standing about ten feet away. She held the dagger in her hand. Kara got up and met her.

"Here. You dropped this after you, uh, dispatched the big guy. That was impressive by the way. I can work with that." She smiled.

"You saved my life. Thank you!"

"Well, you saved mine as well, so we're even." Kara noticed the deep amber eyes when she smiled this time.

"Wait. What do you mean? Work with what? Who are you?" Kara gave a confused look.

"The name's Olivia Ashwood, and we have a lot to talk about."

THE BEGINNING

Kara will return in

THE ASHWOOD CHRONICLES

BOOK 1

THE GUARDIAN

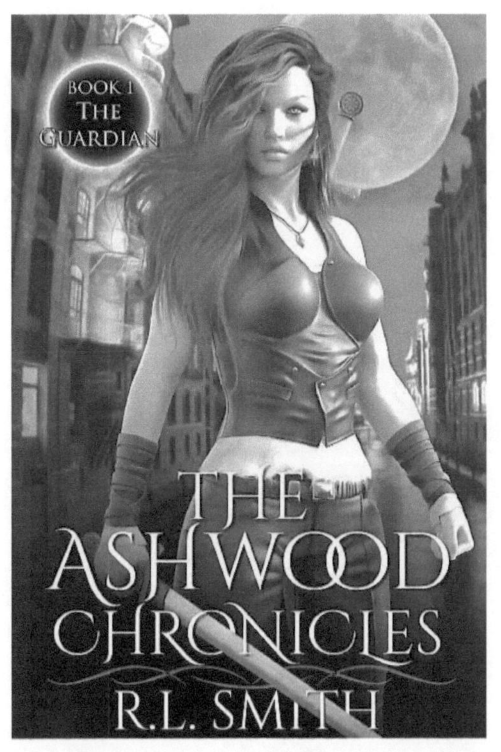

COMING FALL OF 2024!

www.rlsmithbooks.com

If you enjoyed this novella, please consider leaving a review on Amazon. It is a small action on your part that has a big impact for me as an author! Every review is truly appreciated and will help me to bring more of what you love to the market.

Sincerely,

R.L. Smith

R.L. Smith lives in GA with his wife, two daughters, and two dogs. He enjoys reading, writing, and playing music (specifically drums).

ACKNOWLEDGEMENTS

Where do I start? First, I have to thank YHWH for his blessings and the talents that He has given me. Without Him, I can do nothing. Second, I want to thank my wife for supporting me during this process and offering many suggestions to make this story far better than it started out.

Thank you to all of my supporters, whether it's on Facebook, YouTube, or Patreon. I couldn't do this without your support. You all know who you are.

Last but not least, thanks to Clarissa Hamrick and my entire ARC Team. Your dedication as well as your mad proofreading skill is essential.

Thank you!

9 798988 535706